EPPIE M. SAYS...

OLIVIER DUNREA

MACMILLAN PUBLISHING COMPANY   NEW YORK
COLLIER MACMILLAN PUBLISHERS   LONDON

Macmillan Publishing Company, 866 Third Avenue, New York, NY 10022
Collier Macmillan Canada, Inc.
Printed and bound in Hong Kong   First American Edition

10   9   8   7   6   5   4   3   2   1

The text of this book is handlettered by the artist.
The illustrations are rendered in pen-and-ink and watercolor.
Library of Congress Cataloging-in-Publication Data
Dunrea, Olivier. Eppie M. says... / by Olivier Dunrea.
— 1st American ed.   p.   cm.   Summary: Life on the farm is never dull for
Ben, who faithfully follows his big sister's advice in such things as
swallowing a live minnow so he can swim like a fish or washing his face
in raindrops so he will never grow old.
ISBN 0 – 02 – 733205 – 5
[1. Sisters — Fiction. 2. Farm life — Fiction.] I. Title.
PZ7.D922Ep 1990 [E] — dc20   89 – 8134 CIP AC

For Eddy B, Daisy D, and Bridey B

My name is Ben Salem.

My most favorite person in the whole wide world
is my sister Eppie M. She knows how to read.
Eppie M. knows just about everything there is
to know. Even Gran says so.   She says
Eppie M. is a regular Miss Know-It-All.

Eppie M. says if you close your eyes and walk backward you'll end up in Australia.

I tried doing it, but I only ended up in the pig wallow.

Eppie M. says if you hold a goose egg under each arm,
they'll hatch out dinosaurs.

I won't have a dinosaur because my eggs broke.

 Eppie M. says if you put your ear to the ground
you can hear the earthworms digging.

Maybe that's true. But I only got an earful of black ants.

Eppie M. says she can juggle three doll babies
and dance a jig with a pig.

That's not true. I saw her drop one of them.

Eppie M. says if you look real hard in a sheep's mouth
you can see his stomach.

I looked in Zook's mouth, but I didn't see anything
because he chewed my nose.

Eppie M. says that each and every raindrop
has a tiny fairy trapped inside it.

That's why if you wash your face in the raindrops you'll never grow old.

It's true! I do it every time it rains,
and I haven't grown old yet.

Eppie M. says if you swallow a live minnow
you'll swim just like a fish.

I swallowed a live minnow and I still can't swim.
I wonder if I swallowed the wrong kind?

Eppie M. says the Queen of England
is coming to tea soon.

She's probably right. Ma made me
change my dirty underwear
after only wearing it for two weeks.

Eppie M. says if you kiss an old mama pig
right on the nose
you'll turn into a handsome prince.

Eppie M. says babies fall from the sky
on rainy days in September.

That's not true!
Everybody knows babies are found under rocks.

Eppie M. says a mean, ugly monster
sleeps under every boy's bed.

Maybe that's true for other boys. But Percy Blue sleeps
under my bed, and he wouldn't let any monsters
get under there with him.

Right before we go to bed Eppie M. and I say good-night
to the moon. Eppie M. says there's a Man-in-the-Moon
and he watches us all night long while we sleep.

I'm going to stay awake all night
and find out if it's true!